Bandit

In early 2023 we decided to set up a charity
in Monty's name to continue his work.

We know he'd be very proud.

www.themontyproject.org

SPLAT

Cookie

BooP!

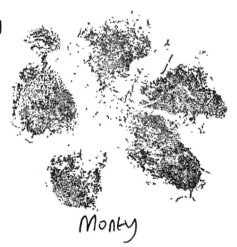

Monty

To Esther

Copyright © M.T. Sanders 2023.

Illustrations by Zoe Saunders.

A CIP catalogue record for this book is available from the British Library.

Paperback ISBN: 978-1-7397049-2-6

This beautiful artwork is by Sienna Rose Crossley
from St. Andrew's C.E. Primary School.

Monty sadly left us in 2022 along with
our beloved spangles Poppy and Bailey.

He leaves behind a wonderful legacy through his stories
and the inspiration he provided for thousands of children.

Monty Dogge,
gone but never forgotten.

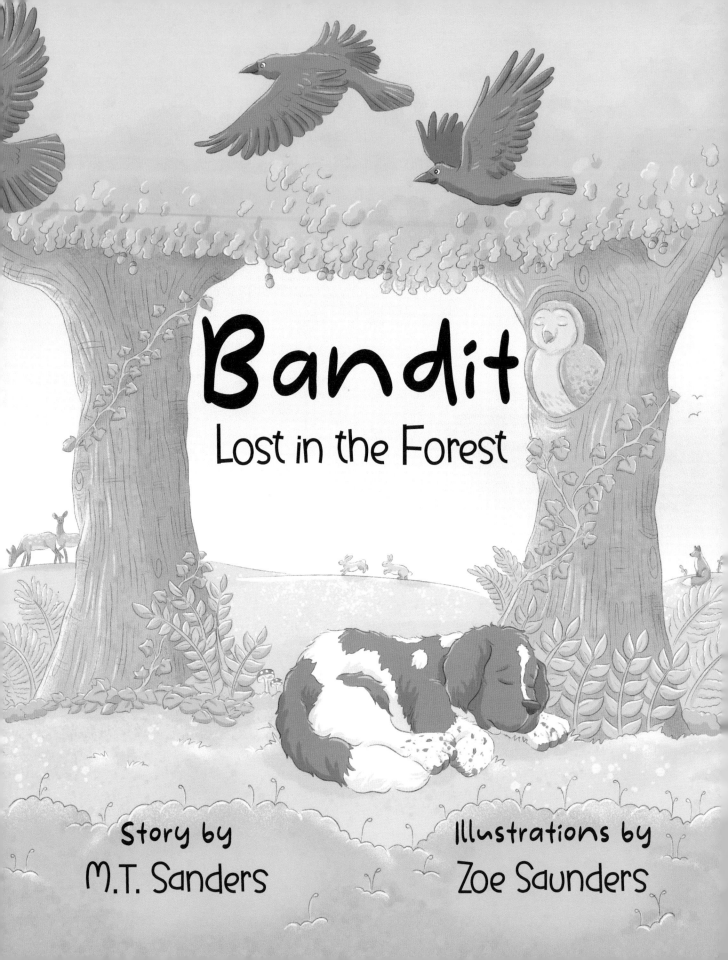

Bandit
Lost in the Forest

Story by
M.T. Sanders

Illustrations by
Zoe Saunders

Early one morning as the forest awoke,
a nut-hunting squirrel neared a mighty great oak.
As he foraged for breakfast a noise made him look up,
and there through the mist lay a Newfydoof pup.

All the great forests creatures soon gathered round,
excited to see what the squirrel had found.
The black and white baby looked confused and afraid.
So the squirrel stepped forward and quietly said...

'Don't be scared little one there is no need for fear.
We'll look after you, you're amongst good friends here.

We must think of a name
because you need one that will fit.'

And he was pleased with their choice.

They named him Bandit.

'We need to find you a home',
said the thoughtful old owl.

I'm sorry I can't help', said the fox with a growl.
'The hunters still come with their horses and hounds,
we need a safe place where he cannot be found.'

Mrs Rabbit stepped forward,
a huge smile on her face.

'We can look after Bandit
we have plenty of space.'

The others agreed and thumped the ground in their glee.
He was pleased with their offer and wagged his tail happily.

But when they got Bandit home, they soon realised,
that small rabbit burrows weren't the ideal size.

Though they pushed really hard they were right out of luck,
the pup was half in and half out and was totally stuck.

A new plan was needed to find Bandit a home.
They couldn't just leave him in the forest alone.
A small herd of deer were just passing through,
and offered a solution about what he could do.

They lived in the forest and not underground.
So no squeezing down holes for this rather large hound.
Bandit was happy but his joy wasn't clear,
because the only thing visible was his big furry rear.

Once released from his jam he quickly followed the herd.
They moved at speed through the forest silently and unheard.
But one really big problem they hadn't given a thought,
is that he couldn't keep up because his legs were too short.

Though he tried really hard he wasn't built like a deer.
This life wasn't for him, that was becoming quite clear.
He went back to the oak, sad and lonely once more.
And sat down dejected on the cold forest floor.

But when it seemed like his hopes
for a new home had sunk.

A friendly face made his way
down the mighty oaks' trunk.

It was the squirrel who had found him in this very same place.
He came right the way down till they sat face to face.

'Don't be sad there my friend I have a place you can stay.
Up there in the branches is our family dray.
It has room for us all and it's comfy and warm,
and built strong to keep out the fiercest storm.'

In what seemed like an instant
and from every direction,
came hundreds of squirrels
with one simple mission.

To help Bandit climb up
to the top of that tree,
where he'd be safe
and secure
with his new family.

'Now if you follow me there,
it's just a short climb.

We'll have you settled at home
in next to no time'.

But try hard as he could
Bandit just got no higher,
the squirrel needed some help
the situation was dire.

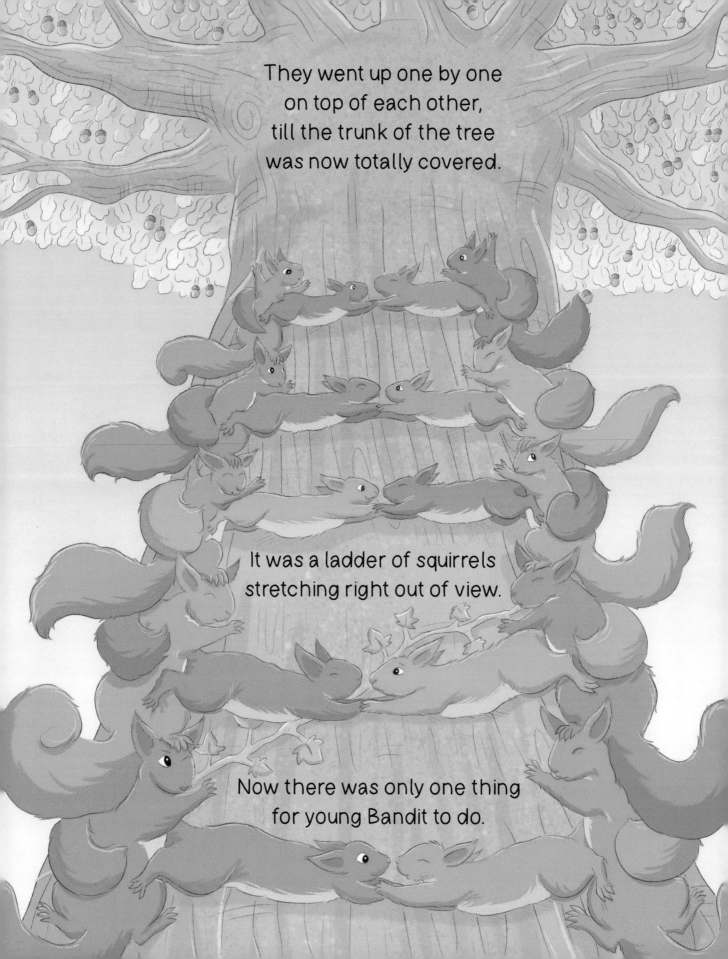

They went up one by one
on top of each other,
till the trunk of the tree
was now totally covered.

It was a ladder of squirrels
stretching right out of view.

Now there was only one thing
for young Bandit to do.

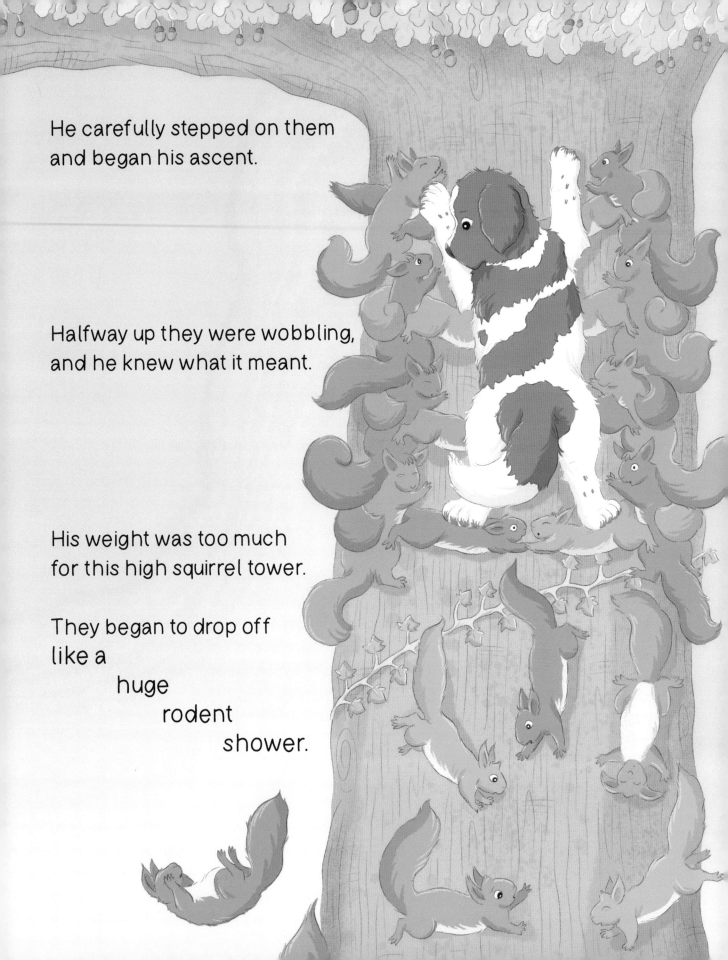

He carefully stepped on them
and began his ascent.

Halfway up they were wobbling,
and he knew what it meant.

His weight was too much
for this high squirrel tower.

They began to drop off
like a
　　　　huge
　　　　　　rodent
　　　　　　　　shower.

Bandit fell with a crash to the forest below,
but as he lay in the leaves little did the pup know,
the creatures were still falling and after a short while,
he'd disappeared completely under a huge squirrel pile.

When finally free the dazed dog was distraught.
This was much harder than anyone thought.

Everyone gathered round and more discussions began.
They chattered together trying to find a new plan.

Almost nobody noticed as the small beaver appeared,
but as it moved forward a way through was cleared.
The beaver addressed them – 'I have an idea.'
He spoke quietly so they all gathered near.

'The pup is a newfydoof', he said to the crowd.
'They are loyal and faithful and have a history that's proud.
The water is the place where Bandit should be,
he'd be welcome to join our small beaver family.'

They all looked at each other and everybody agreed.
This could be the most wonderful idea indeed.

No holes to go down or falling squirrels to dodge.
He'd be all safe and snug in his own beaver lodge.

All was good, things went well. Bandit settled right in.
He enjoyed his new home and all the chances to swim.

He even fetched logs for the beaver's new dam.
He enjoyed helping out every time that he swam.

But Bandit's quiet life was to change without warning,
when a storm hit the forest the very next morning.
The sky became angry and the wind bent the trees.
And the river swirled wildly in the strengthening breeze.

The rain fell like bullets forcing water to rise,
with no break visible from the almost black skies.
The beavers told Bandit that nobody could stay.
Their home was at risk and may be soon swept away.

Bandit was scared because he couldn't swim well,
he'd only just learnt, and the beavers could tell.
They all tried to help him make the opposite bank,
but the water was fierce. They lost their grip and he sank.

The fast-flowing rapids took poor Bandit downstream.
The pup dragged by the currents like some horrible dream.
Though he fought and he struggled it all seemed in vain.
The river was too strong he felt his energy drain.

He
slowly
started
to
sink

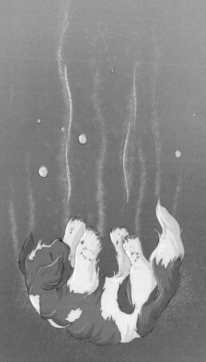

but then from deep down below,
came a light warm and bright
like a massive rainbow.

As it rose, from its beams,
came a wonderful sight.

A huge black and white dog
swam straight up
from the light.

It appeared right below him and it lifted him up,
until it brought to the surface the spluttering pup.
Then to a small and safe island he was gently pushed on,
and as quick as it came the dog and rainbow had gone.

The small pup was exhausted and as he drifted to sleep,
he wondered what had just pulled him from the water so deep.
As dreams danced in his head the evening grew dark,
when he was suddenly awoken by a loud booming bark.

From out of the forest Cookie suddenly appeared.
The storm had now eased, the rain clouds had cleared.
It was quiet and calm after the raging downpour.
She got to the river and walked down to the shore.

As she looked out at the island, she spotted the pup.
Though she barked out a welcome he never looked up.

He was drenched and not moving – she just had to go see.
She swam out to Bandit and brought him back to safety.

When he told her his story about not having a home,
she instantly knew she couldn't leave him alone.
Her family were kind and they had plenty of space.
She knew this would be Bandit's forever place.

He was greeted with love; he was home finally.
With Cookie and the hoomans his new family.

There were adventures to come, and there would be lots.
But his life saved in that river he never forgot.

Cookie told Bandit stories about Monty, her late brother.
He loved to hear all those tales and always asked for another.

With every story he heard Bandit was ever more sure...

That he knew Monty well...

...He'd met him before.

Other Books Available by the Author ...

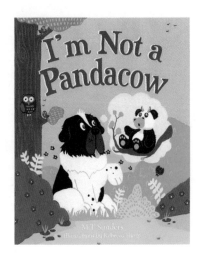

A delightful story about Monty, a huge Newfoundland puppy, and his journey to find out what he is. But will asking the other dogs he meets on his travels give him the answers he wants?

By M.T. Sanders.
With illustrations by Rebecca Sharp.

ISBN 978-1-912014-7-3

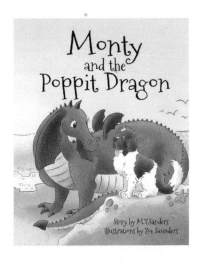

Monty, Cookie and the spangles are off on their holidays to sunny Pembrokeshire and the beautiful beach at Poppit Sands. In a cave they meet a new friend, the Poppit Dragon, who is sad because she can't fly. Can Monty and the gang save the day?

By M.T. Sanders. With illustrations by Zoe Saunders.

ISBN 978-1-912014-06-4

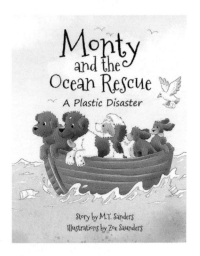

Monty, Cookie and the spangles are back at the beach.When Cookie sees a splash in the water her newfydoof instinct to rescue takes over and she immediately heads out to help.

What follows is an adventure that could turn out to be their biggest, and most difficult so far.

By M.T. Sanders, with illustrations by Zoe Saunders.

ISBN 978-1913071-13-4

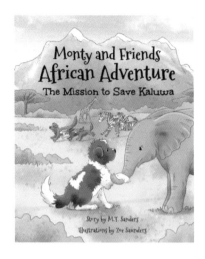

Now famous after their ocean rescue, Monty, Cookie and the spangles were looking forward to a well-earned rest. But when a letter arrives from Africa they need to act fast. Kaluwa a baby Elephant is being held captive and what follows is a race against time to rescue her. But will they be too late?

By M.T. Sanders. With illustrations by Zoe Saunders.

ISBN: 978-1-913071-51-6

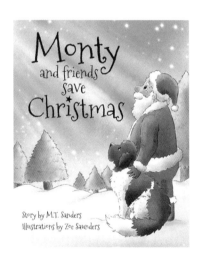

When Santa visits Monty's house, things don't quite go to plan. Cookie has managed to scare the reindeers away and they are nowhere to be seen. Children around the world are waiting, but who will pull the sleigh? It's going to take a massive effort to save Christmas... and time is running out.

A magical festive story of friendship and overcoming the odds.

By M.T. Sanders, with illustrations by Zoe Saunders.

ISBN 978-1912014-41-5

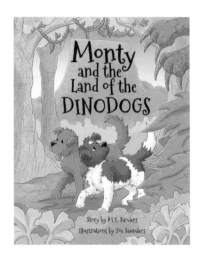

While out in the woods Monty and Cookie stumble upon a strange machine, untouched for years. What follows is a monstrous adventure that will take them back to a time long long ago.

Hold on tight because the excitement has just begun. We're off to a world undiscovered for thousands of years - Welcome to the Land of the Dinodogs!

ISBN 978-1913071-60-8

www.montydogge.com

www.themontyproject.org

Printed in Great Britain
by Amazon